SHAKESPEARE RETOLD

ROMEO
AND JULIET

by

Martin Waddell & Alan Marks

W

FRANKLIN WATTS
LONDON•SYDNEY

First published in 2008
by Franklin Watts
338 Euston Road
London NW1 3BH

Franklin Watts Australia
Level 17/207 Kent Street
Sydney NSW 2000

Text copyright © Martin Waddell 2008
Illustrations copyright © Alan Marks 2008

The rights of Martin Waddell to be identified as the
author and Alan Marks as the illustrator of this
Work have been asserted in accordance with the
Copyright, Designs and Patents Act, 1988.

Editor: Jackie Hamley
Designer: Peter Scoulding

A CIP catalogue record for this book is available
from the British Library.

ISBN: 978 0 7496 7747 3 (hbk)
ISBN: 978 0 7496 7753 4 (pbk)

Printed in China

Fnanklin Watts is a division of
Hachette Children's Books,
an Hachette Livre UK company.
www.hachettelivre.co.uk

CONTENTS

The Cast

Romeo – Old Montague's son
Juliet – Old Capulet's daughter

Old Montague – nobleman of Verona
Lady Montague – his wife
Benvolio – Romeo's friend and cousin
Mercutio – Romeo's friend and kinsman
of the Prince of Verona

Old Capulet – nobleman of Verona
Lady Capulet – his wife
Tybalt – Juliet's cousin
Nurse – Juliet's friend and advisor
Paris – Juliet's suitor and kinsman
of the Prince of Verona

The Prince of Verona
Friar Lawrence – Romeo's friend and advisor

PROLOGUE

A boy and a girl fall in love
despite a family feud. Young men fight,
and wasted blood flows in the street.
A potion causes seeming death.
Poison and a dagger bring a
tragic end when...

Romeo loves Juliet.

CHAPTER ONE

HOT BLOOD

One summer morning, a long time ago,
two gangs met in the streets of Verona.
One boy taunted another, then others
joined in. Stones and insults flew and swords
were drawn before the Prince of Verona's
men stopped the fight.

The Prince of Verona sent for two old
men, Montague and Capulet, whose
followers had been fighting.

"Montague! Capulet!" roared the prince.

Two elderly noblemen faced him, breathing fire.

"This endless feuding between your followers
must stop!" the angry prince ordered.
"If it happens again your lives will be forfeit!
Capulet, come with me! Montague…
I will deal with you later!"

The prince led Capulet away, and old
Montague and his wife turned to their
nephew, Benvolio.

"What happened?" old Montague asked.

"It started with the usual name calling," said
Benvolio. "But that idiot, hot-head Capulet,
Tybalt, attacked me. Then the others joined in."

"I'm glad Romeo wasn't there," said Lady Montague, tired of the old men's quarrel and worried about her son.

"Where is our son? What's wrong with him?" old Montague mused. "Why is he so miserable?"

"I'll find out," Benvolio consoled the old couple and he went to talk to Romeo.

"In love?" Benvolio asked his cousin, though he thought he knew the answer.

"In love... but not loved," Romeo sighed. "Rosaline is the most beautiful girl I have ever seen... but she is not interested in me."

"Use your eyes!" Benvolio told him. "Look at some other girls."

"How could I love some other girl?" Romeo objected.

"The Capulets' feast is this evening," Benvolio grinned. "We could go… many of the guests will be masked, so we won't be recognised. Your beloved Rosaline will be there with all the other beauties of Verona. Compare her with some I'll show you… you'll think your swan a crow!"

The chance of seeing Rosaline was something that Romeo could not resist, no matter what the risk.

TWO LOVERS MEET

That night the Capulets' house glittered with
torchlight. There was music and dancing and
rich food and fine wine. All the noble families
of Verona had been invited, except the
hated Montagues.

Romeo searched the crowd for a glimpse of
Rosaline, but Benvolio was beginning to feel
uneasy. *What if Tybalt sees us?* he thought.

"Benvolio?" Someone tapped his shoulder
from behind. Benvolio whirled round. It was
his friend Mercutio, a kinsman of the prince.

"Have you come to dance with Tybalt?"
Mercutio grinned. "Be careful...
he's coming this way."

"We'd better leave, now!" Benvolio told Romeo.

"Not till I've seen Rosaline!" Romeo objected, but he didn't find Rosaline. Instead he saw the most beautiful girl in the world.

She smiled… she was smiling at him!
He knew it.

"I never saw true beauty till this night!" Romeo
exclaimed, his dreams of Rosaline forgotten.

Tybalt heard… and
recognised Romeo.
"That villain Montague!"
he swore angrily,
"Let me at him!"

Old Capulet stopped
Tybalt. "This is my house
and Romeo is now a
guest, nephew!" he said.

"I'm not standing for this!"
the angry Tybalt swore.

"I am master here!
You will obey me!" old
Capulet snapped back.

A furious Tybalt stalked
from the room.

Romeo met the girl who had enchanted him. They spoke only a few words, but it was enough. With the excitement of the wine and the music and the dancing and the torchlight, those few words led instantly to love. Entranced with each other, their hands touched, briefly, and that fleeting touch seemed like a kiss.

Juliet's old nurse bustled between them.
"Madam, your mother calls you!" the old woman
said. The girl moved reluctantly away, her gaze
still fixed on Romeo.

"Who is that girl?" Romeo asked the nurse.

"That's my dove, my darling, sweet Juliet,
the daughter of this house!" the giddy
old nurse smiled, flouncing after the girl.

"My love... a Capulet!" groaned
Romeo.

"Who is that boy?" Juliet pleaded.

"That's Romeo," the nurse
frowned. "Montague's son!"

"That I must love a loathed
enemy," Juliet whispered
to herself, half in joy, half
in despair.

CHAPTER THREE

ROMEO AND JULIET

When the festivities ended, Romeo did not go home with the others. Instead, he climbed over the high wall that surrounded the Capulets' garden, and hid, hoping to see Juliet.

She came out on to a balcony, framed in the light from her bedroom. Her coming seemed like the rising of the sun to Romeo.

"Why must he be a Montague!" she spoke out loud. "What's in a name? A rose called by any other name would smell as sweet. I love Romeo!"

Juliet loves me! Romeo thought, calling her name, softly.

"Romeo!" the girl gasped. "Romeo, if my family were to find you here... "

"Love brought me here!" he told her. "Love knows no fear."

"You heard me say I love you... though you were not meant to hear me speak those words, not yet!" the girl blushed. "If you love me too... say so!"

"I swear it by the moon!" he told her.

"The moon comes and goes," she said. "What kind of love is that?"

"What shall I swear by?" the boy smiled. "You are my dear love... "

Then they heard the nurse calling Juliet's name.

"We must exchange vows!" Romeo urged her. "We must marry."

"You have my vow of love already," she whispered. "But if you mean what you say, and we are to marry... we must marry soon, or our families will stop us."

"Tomorrow! Send a messenger to me... I'll find a way!" Romeo told her.

"Parting is such sweet sorrow," she sighed. "I'll say goodnight... until tomorrow!"

Romeo went to his old friend and advisor, Friar Lawrence. He lived outside the city walls, surrounded by the herbs he gathered for his potions.

"You... old Montague's son, want to marry Capulet's daughter?" the friar gasped.

"It must be done today, quickly... or our families will stop us!" Romeo insisted and the reluctant friar allowed himself to be persuaded.

Juliet's giddy nurse was easily convinced to act as go between. She knew that the Capulets planned to marry their daughter to the prince's kinsman, Paris... but surely her darling should marry for love?

For love of love, the excited old woman conspired with the friar, arranging the time and place of the marriage. She hurried back to tell Juliet what was planned.

That afternoon, Romeo and Juliet were married secretly by Friar Lawrence.

Maybe their love will end the feud!
the friar thought, hopefully.

Maybe... or maybe not.

CHAPTER FOUR

BLOOD FLOWS

Meanwhile Romeo's friends Benvolio and Mercutio were idling in the hot streets, knowing nothing of Romeo and Juliet's secret marriage.

"We should go indoors," Benvolio warned. "For I know your temper, Mercutio. If we meet Tybalt again after last night…"

"My temper!" Mercutio laughed. "I've seen you start an argument because someone coughed in the street!"

Just then Tybalt came on the scene. Still angry about what had happened at the feast, he was hunting the streets for Romeo.

"I do not like the company you keep!" Tybalt sneered at Mercutio, trying to pick a fight. At that moment Romeo appeared, still in his dream of love.

"Romeo!" roared Tybalt, paying no more attention to Mercutio.

"We have no quarrel!" Romeo told him, drawing back. All his thoughts were of Juliet. How could he love one Capulet, and fight another?

But if Romeo was unwilling to face Tybalt, the hot-tempered Mercutio wasn't. He drew his sword and faced Tybalt.

Romeo tried to come between his friend and Juliet's cousin to stop them fighting, but in the struggle Tybalt's sword clashed with Romeo's and pierced Mercutio's body.

"A plague on both your houses," Mercutio groaned, dying in Benvolio's arms.

Romeo froze, not knowing
what to do, but then
he found himself facing
the enraged Tybalt.
"Scum of a Montague!"
Tybalt swore.

Romeo's blood
boiled. In the heat
of the moment, he
thought of nothing
but avenging the
death of his friend.

They fought...
and Tybalt died.

"Oh, I am fortune's fool!"
Romeo groaned, realising
what he had done.

"Leave now, before the
prince hears of this!"
Benvolio insisted.

Romeo quickly escaped
from the city, leaving
Benvolio to face the
Montagues and
the Capulets...
and the prince.

Romeo made his way to Friar Lawrence,
hoping that the old priest might
be able to help.

"The prince has accepted Benvolio's
version of what happened," the friar told
Romeo. "He will be merciful. You will
not be executed, but you must never
return to Verona. If you do... you die.
That is the law. Juliet mourns her
cousin Tybalt... but she still loves
you despite Tybalt's dying by
your hand. Go to her
tonight, as you had
planned. Then
leave Verona
forever."

That night Romeo
returned to the city in
secret and made his
way to the Capulets'
garden. He climbed up
to the balcony where
Juliet stood waiting
for him.

Romeo and Juliet spent their
wedding night together,
though they had to part
when the lark sang
at dawn.

"We will be together
again somehow.
Trust me," said Romeo,
as he bade her farewell.

Then it all went
horribly wrong.

CHAPTER FIVE

THE FRIAR'S PLAN

"We know you mourn for your cousin Tybalt," old Capulet told Juliet. "But you are too young to live in sorrow. Be happy... you are to marry the prince's kinsman, Paris."

"I... I can't," Juliet gasped.

"You can and you will... or you are no daughter of mine!" old Capulet swore.

"Forget Romeo!" her nurse insisted. "No one will ever know what passed between you. Paris will make you happy!"

In despair, Juliet went to Friar Lawrence. "What can I do?" she asked. "I cannot marry Paris. I love Romeo, and I am married to him."

The friar tried to help the weeping girl. "I will prepare a potion for you," he told her. "Drink it tonight, before you sleep. You will sleep... but it will look as if you have died. They will lay you in the family vault. After two days, you will wake. I will send a messenger to Romeo to make sure he is there when you awake. Then the two of you can leave Verona, and be together."

Juliet returned home and, to the delight of her parents, agreed to the marriage with Paris. Then she quickly excused herself – supposedly to prepare for her wedding day.

Fearing that the potion would kill her but with her heart filled with love for Romeo, Juliet did as the friar told her.

She seemed dead when the nurse came to wake her. As the friar had predicted, she was laid in the family vault by her grieving father and Lady Capulet.

CHAPTER SIX

A DEATHLY SLEEP

The plan might have worked...
but news of Juliet's death
reached Romeo before the
friar's message. "I must be
with her!" the griefstricken
Romeo cried. He bought a
draught of poison and hurried
back to Verona.

As the unhappy Romeo broke
into the Capulets' vault, he
was interrupted. Paris had
set his heart on marrying
Juliet. Now the girl he loved
was dead, and he had come
to mourn her, leaving his
servant at the gate to see
that he was not disturbed.

"A murdering Montague breaking into Capulets' holy ground!" Paris swore when he saw Romeo. His grief turned to rage, and he drew his sword.

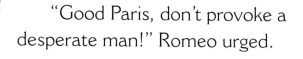

"Good Paris, don't provoke a desperate man!" Romeo urged.

The grieving Paris lunged at Romeo. They fought... and Paris died.

"You lie there, killed by a man who is dead himself," Romeo groaned, looking down at Paris.

He turned to the marble bier where Juliet's body lay veiled. "Oh my love, my wife!" he whispered, folding the veil back to gaze upon her face. Then he drank the poison he had brought. "Here's to my love!" Romeo sighed, as he died.

The friar entered the vault, too late. He saw the stains of Paris' blood and discovered his body and that of Romeo.

Juliet stirred, her eyes opening. "Romeo! Where is Romeo?" she sighed. Then she saw his body.

The friar had only one thought. The city watchmen, alerted by Paris' servant, would soon be on their way. "We must leave this place," he urged Juliet. "I'll find somewhere where you can be safe."

Juliet refused. "I shall not leave!" she told him.

Alone after the friar
had gone, she knelt
beside Romeo's body.
She kissed him gently,
hoping that poison lingered
on his lips, so that she might
die as well.

"Your lips are warm," she
said, softly stroking his face,
but death did not come to her
with the kiss.

She drew the
dagger from
Romeo's belt.

"Dagger, this is your
sheath," she sighed,
thrusting it into her heart.
"Rest there, and let me die."

So young love ended.

Old Montague and old Capulet were left to mourn their children. They did so in peace, but this peace between them had been bought at a terrible price.

"Never was there a story of more woe, than this of Juliet and her Romeo," the prince told the old men.

And they wept together.

EPILOGUE

Poison and a dagger
ended a forbidden love but...

Romeo loved Juliet.

Born to hate, they loved instead.

NOTES

by Dr Catherine Alexander

The story of Romeo and Juliet was already well known through English, French and Italian novels and poems when Shakespeare wrote his play, probably in 1594 or 1595. But it is his version that has become best known and most popular.

Romeo and Juliet opens with a prologue that tells the plot of the play. It may seem odd that Shakespeare gives the game away at the beginning by announcing what will happen, but it is worth remembering that the story was already well known. The interest for the reader or the audience was to find out what Shakespeare did with the story and how he was going to treat this material.

The play has remained popular because it deals with matters that are still important and interesting over four hundred years after it was written. It also contains some of the most memorable moments and scenes that Shakespeare ever created.

And there is a dilemma – a moral problem – at the heart of the play. Romeo and Juliet are very young to fall in love and get married (Juliet is not quite fourteen) and both of them ought to obey their parents. Had they done so they would not have died. It is their suicides, however, which bring an end to the 'ancient grudge' in Verona and unite the Montagues and Capulets, so perhaps some good comes from their tragedy.

The play asks if it is right to put love before other considerations. Are Romeo and Juliet selfish or should they follow where their emotions lead them?

At the start of the play Romeo is in love with Rosaline but switches very suddenly to Juliet when he sees her at the Capulets' ball. Does this suggest that he is fickle and unreliable? And is Juliet old enough to know what is best for her? Shakespeare makes them very attractive and sympathetic characters but that doesn't make their behaviour right.

On the other hand, they don't have much help or guidance – they are on their own. They are let down by their parents, who have other plans for their future. Romeo's friends belong to the gangs that are causing trouble in the city. Juliet doesn't have friends but is very close to her nurse who doesn't give her the best advice. The churchman, Friar Lawrence, is on their side and tries to help but his plans only make matters worse.

Some of the saddest and most painful parts of the play (and this is Shakespeare's great skill) are the number of 'if only' moments: if only Benvolio hadn't persuaded Romeo to go to the Capulets' feast; if only Romeo hadn't fought and killed Tybalt; if only Friar Lawrence's message had got to Romeo;

if only Juliet had woken from the poison before Romeo thought she was dead.

The play would have been very different – and not nearly as memorable or famous – if Shakespeare had made different choices.

ROMEO AND JULIET FACTS

❖ It is the most famous love story
in the world – perhaps in history –
and has been turned into many
films (at least 23 and in many
different languages), ballets,
musicals and operas. The focus
is often on the feuding gangs
and families (*West Side Story*,
1961, for example).

❖ In 1986 Michael Bogdanov directed
a modern-dress *Romeo and Juliet* for the Royal
Shakespeare Company with an Italian setting.
Tybalt drove a bright red sports car and the
production became known as the 'Alfa-Romeo
and Juliet'.

❖ There has even been an animated film based
loosely on the play which features the Montagues
and Capulets as seals!